Rock Chalk Dreams

Adapted from "Cuddy's Baby"

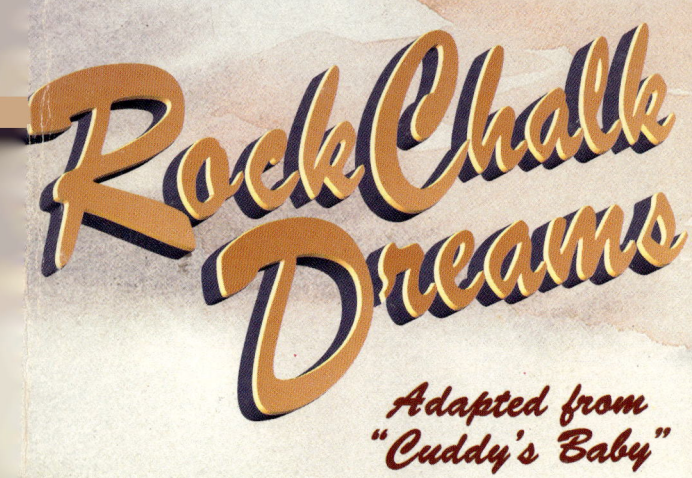

Margaret Hill McCarter

Rock Chalk Dreams

Adapted from "Cuddy's Baby"

Margaret Hill McCarter

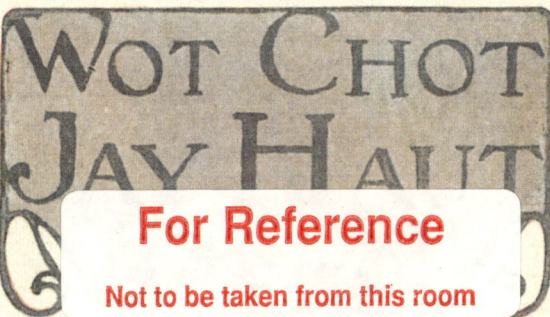

ISBN 0-9649023-0-3

Copyright © 1995

Introductory section written by
Merlyn Louis Brown

Reproductions of original paintings by
Ernst Ulmer

Original text reproduced from
"Cuddy's Baby" by Margaret Hill McCarter

Published by
Historic Adventures Publishing and
Merlyn Louis Brown

INTRODUCTION

"Rock chalk, Jayhawk, Daddy. Say it Daddy." The voice was that of two year old Spencer sleeping at the foot of our bed. I laughed and asked him why he wanted me to say that. No reply. I rolled out of bed, put my hand on his tiny shoulder. He was still asleep. It was apparent that the spell of the mythical red and blue bird known as a Jayhawk, unique to the Midwest, had taken an early hold on this tow-headed Kansas boy.

Apparently, this was not an isolated incident. The Rock Chalk chant seems to have a magic about it. It invades the dreams of children; it plants hope in those far too young to entertain desires of a higher education; its strained chords apparently reverberate around the world.

Within the pages of this book is the story of another little Kansas boy who, at the age of four, incidentally was introduced to the chant even before the mythical bird arrived. The chant, which evolved from "Rah, Rah Jayhawk" in 1886 to "Rock Chalk, Jayhawk" around the turn of the century, so enthralled little Harold Perine

one day that it became his inspiration and, many times, his most vital form of communication. The first Jayhawk did not even land on Henry Maloy's sketch pad until 1912, too late to decorate the child's hat or scarf, but not too late to touch the child with its apparently omnipresent ability to induce hope and excitement.

Of course, the author of this magnificent rendering of a struggle between man and the elements would be the first to dispel the theory of a mystical presence of an omnipresent bird and the coincidence of this seemingly random event.

Instead, she would, posthumously if she could (and really she does in this book), tell you that baby Harold and his mother were the salt of the earth, whom the Master took special care to preserve and enhance so that they might be an antiseptic for the ills of others and a tasteful enhancement to their world.

The author would also tell you that the sun's rays were the arms of God reaching out to a needy world and that the troubles of the early prairie were burdens which, if lifted up to the Master, would become wings to lift the bearer to new heights. There were no random events and no coincidental meetings. This was God's plan for Harold Perine.

The author would not, however, for one minute deny the power of an education, the almost mystical persuasion of the Jayhawk, and the spiritually uplifting significance of the Rock Chalk Chant. They all played important roles in baby Harold's life much as they have for many of us.

ABOUT THE AUTHOR

Margaret Hill McCarter was a noted author and a leader in the women's suffrage movement. The Topeka schoolteacher gained national notoriety when she became the first woman to ever address a Republican National Convention in 1920. She argued nationally for the right of women to vote but fought just as vociferously for their right to keep their age a secret at the polls. She was also a leader in the prohibition movement.

Born to Quaker parents near Charlottesville, Indiana, May 2, 1860, Mrs. McCarter moved to Topeka, Kansas, in 1888 to become an English instructor after 15 years as a public school teacher in her home state. She lived in Topeka until her death at the age of 78.

Mrs. McCarter's literary career began with several short stories around the turn of the century and ended after publishing more than a dozen books, mostly about life on the early frontier. Among her published works were: "The Cottonwoods' Story," "Cuddy," "Cuddy's Baby," "In Old Quivera," "Peace of the Solomon Valley," "A Wall of Men," "Master's Degree," "Winning the Wilderness," Vanguards of the Plains," "The Reclaimers," "Widening Waters," "The Corner Stone," "Paying Mother," "Homeland," "The Candle in the Window," and "The Price of the Prairie."

Confining her stories to family life on the prairie, Mrs. McCarter once boasted that "I never dipped my pen in slime or wrote anything my children might read and wish mother had not written."

Historic Adventures Publishing is proud to present this reprint of one of Margaret Hill McCarter's finest treasures, hidden for a period of time, but now unveiled as "Rock Chalk Dreams."

ABOUT THIS BOOK

When I first read "Cuddy's Baby" I knew the words had a life beyond the apparent grave to which the rare edition had been subjected. The book was initially written by Margaret Hill McCarter, a Topeka school teacher, and copyrighted by Topeka's Crane and Company shortly after the turn of the century. The particular edition that I inherited had been republished with additional color graphics by a Chicago publishing company and sold under the same name. Because of the wisdom found in America's copyright laws, it is now possible to republish this rare treasure and share my wonderful inheritance with you the reader.

Judging from the signing of her maiden name, my grandmother had kept her particular volume of "Cuddy's Baby" since shortly after publication. Before Grandmother Tipp's death in 1989 I was asked what I would like as my inheritance. I simply told my grandmother that I would take what no one else wanted. I said I wouldn't mind having the books if no one else cared about them.

A year or so later my mother, having remembered my request, handed me perhaps the best hidden treasure a journalist could uncover: a rare edition book with a beloved subject set in a beloved time and a beloved place. But, much more than that, this book contained a dream that wouldn't die for its characters, and resurrecting its message became a dream that wouldn't die for me.

There was a lot of Cuddy's baby's dreams in this boy from rural Kansas. We shared a love for the University of Kansas and we shared a desire to get an education to enhance our power over our circumstances. And, evidently, we shared a heritage of familial love and individual determination.

The publishing of "Rock Chalk Dreams" and the commissioning of the painting "Rock Chalk Preview" was birthed of that heritage. For four or five years I sought a way to bring the story to life. In 1993 I arranged a meeting with artist Ernst Ulmer. I fell in love with his presentation of history on canvass and knew he was a part of the picture. Two years later, Mr. Ulmer, an internationally acclaimed artist, was commissioned to bring the opening scene of the book to life. Mr. Ulmer researched the setting to make the scene historically accurate. I made a few scratches on paper that vaguely represented my dream of how the painting should look.

How can we feature the baby? How did the campus look at the time? How can we accurately depict literature and history while making it artistically pleasing? Can it be done?

"Absolutely" was the answer as oils brushed literature to life on clay in the Ulmer studio. The result was a beautiful limited edition lithograph which we titled "Rock Chalk Preview" because the scene depicted the setting for baby Harold's preview to an education and a better life.

One of the stages of an artist's commissioning process is to provide the client with a "proof" print so that client and artist might agree on the work before the full-size production begins. We chose our proof print for the cover of this book, not only to display more of Mr. Ulmer's talent, but to also allow you, the reader, to be a part of the wonderful process that led to the fulfillment of this dream.

We hope you enjoy the artist's work, the author's work, and we hope, by purchasing this book and/or lithograph, you will enjoy being a part of our own Rock Chalk Dreams. It is truly a unique "mixed medium" of art, history, and literature.

DEDICATION

To the author, Margaret Hill McCarter, whose words painted incredible scenes of prairie life and whose deeds left an amazing legacy as an activist for women's suffrage and other issues of her time. May this edition carry her legacy even further.

"Rock Chalk Dreams" is also dedicated to my grandmother, Chelsea (Long) Tipp, who like the author was a one-room schoolhouse teacher and evidently shared the author's love for poetry and prose. Grandma never threw a book away and much as baby Harold "incidentally" was introduced to an "edication," the book "Cuddy's Baby" was introduced to me as it was handed down through the family.

I'm sure that my grandparents found hope in spite of their struggles on their farm in north-central Kansas in much the same way Cuddy and her baby Harold found hope in the story told between the covers of this book.

And I know, beyond a shadow of a doubt, that all of them were, as Margaret Hill McCarter described them, those of whom the Master spoke when he said: "Ye are the salt of the earth."

Thanks to my own Cuddy, Mary Lou Brown, for passing this book along and for inspiring me to my own education.

And, whether you graduated from the University of Kansas, Harvard, or the University of Hawaii, if you've only been able to hope for an education or if you have a doctorate, or if you simply have daily struggles trying to make ends meet, this story is for you.

It's really not so much a story about a chant as it is about the spirit of hope that comes from the chant. It's not so much about a particular university as it is about the power and freedom that can be derived from a good education. And it is not so much about one family's struggles against the elements as it is about all of our struggles in life.

May we all hold on to our Rock Chalk Dreams, and, in the spirit of "Cuddy's Baby," never, absolutely never, give up!

Rock Chalk, Jayhawk. K. Uo-o-o!

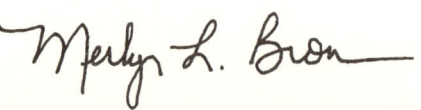

There are about two billions of *people* holding down the earth's crust under the special dispensation of gravitation, but you and I, my dear reader, will never know more than a tiny group of them until they cease to be *people* and become *folks* to us. Then they enter into our day's work and are forevermore a part of its machinery.

Cuddy and her baby were only *folks,* and I am telling you their story because, in the length and breadth of things, I believe they may have been among those to whom the Master spoke when He said: *"Ye are the salt of the earth."*

I
The Game

Cuddy's Baby

I

THE GAME

There's a breathless hush in the Close tonight—
  Ten to make, and the match to win—
A bumping pitch, and a blinding light,
  An hour to play and the last man in.
And it's not for the sake of a ribboned coat,
  Or the selfish hope of a season's fame,
But his Captain's hand on his shoulder smote—
  "Play up! play up! and play the game!"
—Henry Newbolt.

"ROCK Chalk! Jay Hawk! K. U-o-o-o!" The long vibrant volume of voices rolled out over the prairie, dying away in a diffusion of atoms of sound with atoms of silence. "Rock Chalk! Jay Hawk! K. U-o-o-o!" Again and again it rose increasingly with the swelling waves of air and pulsed out softly into that weird cadence that carries "the lost chord" in its ebbing tones. The November day was clear and still. The winds of heaven moved gently, and the landscape lay under the benediction of quietness. It was one of the last days of a gorgeous Indian summer in Kansas which makes up for the lack of the beautiful foliage tints of the Eastern States in the resplendent richness of its skies, and the soft indeterminate hues of its broad reach of distances. The late afternoon sun was slipping down the west into a sea of glass mingled with fire.

Out beyond the little city, under the shadow of the hill-slope, was an athletic field where on this November afternoon the grand-stand was packed, and the open spaces were lined with an expectant crowd watching a great football struggle. The day before, a high wind had carried down a long section of fence-screen built above the tight ground fence to shut off the view of the park from the hill-slope up which the roadway ran. A jam of buggies, carriages, and farm wagons (there were no automobiles then) filled the road, leaving no space for those who would pass on their way. Caught in the jam was an old one-horse wagon, whose driver, a plain farmer, would have hurried on. He had a good-natured, patient face where the lines that disappointment and failure had graven had not barred out determination and hope. Finding no way out of the crowd, whose interest made them forget everything else, the man in the wagon turned to his wife sitting beside him.

"We may just as well wait, Mother," he said cheerily. "This is one of

Cuddy's Baby 3

them football games the University's goin' wild about. Looks like prize-fightin' to me. If that's eddication I don't want none. Them colleges has both come here to play today on account of all gettin' to go to the opery tonight an' hearin' that great singer, I'll never tell you her name."

"It's not eddication, Joe Perine," replied his wife. "It's anything but that, it seems to me. I don't like to see it, and yit it's fascinatin', too."

"Neither do I, an' I want to be gettin' home, but we'll have to wait."

He settled himself, patiently indifferent to the game, and began to study the people in the variety of vehicles about him. Mrs. Perine did the same—just a poor farmer and his wife getting home from a trip to town.

Hard work had made them both look older than they really were—the hard work the Kansas farmers knew who struggled to make homes for themselves in the time when the raw beginnings of the State, though past its days of ruffianism, required every man to be a hero. Seated between the two was little Harold Perine, a sturdy baby boy of four years. His cheeks were rosy, his fair hair curled softly about his head, his eyes were deeply blue like his mother's. In fact, his whole face was hers recast in baby mold. With wide-open eyes he watched the game, seeing every little detail as only a child can see. It was so utterly strange to him, the crowded grand-stand, the side-lines black with spectators, and in the open the contending teams forging back and forth across the gridiron spaces.

"Rock Chalk! Jay Hawk! K. U-o-o!" again and again the shout went up with its tremendous surge of sound.

"What for they say 'at?" asked the little one.

"Oh, that's to keep their courage up, I guess, Baby, and help them to win," answered his mother, more to satisfy him than from any definite knowledge.

"Is they p'ayin' bat-man?" he questioned.

"No, no, they are playin' football, not black-man."

Baby Harold watched more intently than ever, noting how, every time the boys from the far side were driven back ever so little, the grand-stand broke into that fierce, fascinating call. His heart began to beat in sympathy with them. Unconsciously he shoved with all the strength of his tiny body against his mother, as if he would help to hold back this enemy to "Rock Chalk." Closer and closer the University's opponents came, fighting foot by foot for the space. Again and again the supporters gave their cry of cheer

Cuddy's Baby 5

and encouragement, till suddenly all was still. Nearer and nearer to the side of the field next to the high roadway the big fellows were driven, and the people held their breath.

"Looks like K. U.'s goin' under," said a big man standing up in a hay-wagon, turning to the shorter ones below him.

Baby Perine's heart gave a great throb. He had caught the spirit of the game. He wondered why the crowd did not call now when there was such need for it. He listened breathless for their cry, and they would not give it. It was the supreme moment. The University eleven were braced for their last stand. There was a deathlike stillness. The very air was motionless.

Suddenly a clear baby voice rang out so sweet and shrill that, from its height on the hill-slope, it reached even the breathless spectators far across the field.

"Wot Chot! Jay Haut! Ta O-o!"

The effect was magical. The crowd went wild. The grand-stand rocked and the fences swayed with the surging shouts of those pressing against them. Down the field went the K. U. men, fierce and furious. Defeat was turning to victory. The wagons on the roadway shifted, and Joe Perine, seeing an opening, hurried his horse through it, and in a minute or two he was out of the jam and on his way toward home.

"I ist wanted to help," said Baby Harold, turning to his mother.

"Well, I reckon you done it, Baby," chuckled Joe. "You'll have to go to the University when you grow up."

"What's the vus'ty, Mamma?" asked Baby.

"It's a place where you yell 'Rock Chalk' if you want to git through," said his father, laughing.

But Mrs. Perine's face had a serious look.

"I'll tell you about it after-while, Baby," she said.

The wagon rattled along the smooth road on to the swell known as Basher's Hill, from the top of which the whole countryside unrolled in the grandeur of a rose-tinged prairie twilight. As the November evening grew chill, Baby Harold nestled down between his father and mother, who drew the old quilt that served for a lap robe snugly about him. With childish joy he crowed and prattled, while from his little muffled-up space every now and then came the glad outburst:

"Wot Chot! Jay Haut! Ta O-o!"

Over the divide and down the long south slope went the Perines, coming at the dusk of evening to the poor little farm-house nestling under the shelter of tall cottonwoods and leaf-stripped elms. There were masses of white and gold chrysanthemums about the kitchen door. The dead vines at the windows and over the crazy little front veranda, and the brown stalks and withered leaves in their rude beds gave ample proof of

> The fair democracy of flowers
> That equals cot and palace,

and that must have made a summertime beauty about the otherwise barren and humble surroundings of a barren and comfortless home.

Some years before Joe Perine and his wife had come with their two little boys to Kansas. They had little capital besides youth and health and ambition. They had little education in books, for both had come from hard-working families, where opportunities were few. But they were intelligent, honest, cheerful, and God-fearing; and combining with these a patient industry, they were representatives of the class that first tilled the Kansas soil and by their own sacrifice sent out a generation of abler men and women to follow them.

The quarter-section of land the Perines had preempted had the inevitable mortgage nailed fast to it, and Joe had little money to pay for help, and little time for anything but the grind of labor. And while annual cultivation was helping the soil to surer crops, the growing bunch of cattle promised a little cut in the mortgage, and the hay in the upland ricks would pay a portion of the December taxes, it was all a slow, back-breaking business; and only Joe Perine's spirit of determination kept him sometimes from utter defeat.

"When we git the land clear we'll fix up the house, Mother," Joe would say encouragingly, and his wife would smile hopefully.

Mrs. Perine had a face an artist could have made into a Madonna's on canvas, had she only been reared in the bounds of luxury. Deep-blue eyes, wavy brown hair, and a fair clear skin; there was an innate refinement about her, a sweetness of expression, a quick intelligence. Some women there are who make any place look more interesting. Mrs. Perine was such a woman. There was a cleanliness about her, and a personality that made one somehow, *feel* her presence. But her manner was simple, and her dress was the plain home-sewed garment of the Kansas country-woman before the days of R. F. D's and rural telephones and King-dragged roads, and low-priced good magazines. She had determination, too, like her husband, but an inborn love of beautiful things, which she could not have, made a void in her life of which he never dreamed.

So, busy as she was, she trained her vines and filled her dooryard with flowers, and patiently replanted what the chickens scratched out, and worked and waited, looking forward to the time when a better house and better fences and bluegrass and blossoms, and a little leisure for books, of which she was fond, might make life more comfortable.

The winter after Harold was born had been a bitterly cold one in Kansas, and the Perine home was not thick-walled against it. The earlier builders in the West were deceived by the warm springs and hot summers and late mild autumns into the belief that the winters were never severe. So they built poorly, both for themselves and their stock.

But there was more than cold that invaded the little dwelling under the cottonwoods that winter. Pneumonia came also. And one black day, when the sunshine lay like a mockery on the desolate prairies, the kindly neighbors had gone with the poor father and mother to where in the new graveyard a wide short grave opened to receive two little forms, and only Baby Harold was left in the dreary Perine home.

How his parents feared for him and clung to him! But he grew chubby and sturdy, filling the house with sunshine as only a baby can. Nothing troubled him. No disease could fasten on him. He was the joy of their lives, the blessing of the days when heart-break slowly gave place to resignation.

On this November evening after Baby had watched his first college game, he trotted to and fro after his mother as she prepared supper.

"What's a vus'ty, Mamma?" he asked again.

"Oh, it's something nice," replied his mother, busy with her duties.

"I wish I had a vus'ty. Tould I eat it, or play wiz it? Is it pwetty? What *is* a vus'ty? 'Wot Chot, Jay Haut, Ta O-o,'" so he prattled on. "Tell me about the vus'ty. I *do* want to know."

But the many evening chores were crowding her, so Baby left her for a little while. At supper in his high chair, as soon as his father had asked the blessing, he broke out in his high clear baby voice, with the new words he had learned.

"Baby will be a singer, some day, like you, Joe," said Mrs. Perine, noting the sweetness and volume of voice with which her darling repeated the call first heard that day by the side of the football field.

Joe Perine was a born singer. His clear tenor voice had been the greatest help the little schoolhouse church at Deer Creek had known. He had never had any training outside of the rural singing-schools of his boyhood. But there was a rich fullness in his tones not often heard in the tenor voice. His baby was already learning to sing — and his

voice had that sweet magnetic tone that makes one listen.

It was late that night before the chores were all done, and the little family sat for a brief time about the kitchen stove. Baby was close in his mother's arms, his chubby hands now and then stroking her cheeks.

"What's a vus'ty, Cuddy-Mamma?" he asked softly.

That was the baby name by which he loved to call her when he was cuddled in her arms at night.

"Baby wouldn't understand," she said. "The University is for boys when they are big. It makes 'em know lots of things."

"How to p'ay bat-man way down by the bid fence?" he queried.

"Yes, and learn books."

"Pwetty pitcher books?"

"Some of them, maybe," said his mother.

"May I have a vus'ty when I det a bid man, an' p'ay bat-man wiz bid mens, an' have books, an' say 'Wot Chot, Jay Haut, Ta O-o'?"

His mother looked at him thoughtfully.

"I'm afraid not, Baby. The University is for folks that have money." The weight of poverty was on her soul as she spoke. "I wish you could go, but I don't know."

"Oh, no," broke in his father, "you'll

Cuddy's Baby 13

be Papa's big boy an' plow an' herd the cattle an' cut the hay. You can drive *two* horses then. You don't want no University."

"Yes, I do," said Baby with quivering lip. "I do want a vus'ty, Papa. Why tan't I have a vus'ty, Cuddy-Mamma? An' when sompin' doin' to det me I'll ist yell 'Wot Chot! Wot Chot!' an' wun fast away. An when I'm 'fwaid in the bid old dark I'll ist say 'Ta O-o!' an' you'll hear me an' help me. I want a vus'ty, Cuddy."

"Poor little feller," said Joe. "Don't cry. You will be Papa's nice big boy, an' maybe — who knows?" He looked at his wife. "Our boy might some day be a scholar."

A look of love shone in the mother's eyes. A shadowy hope for impossible things. The long mortgage debt, the taxes and interest, the stretching of every penny that did not allow even the necessities of life, how could schooling that cost money ever be their baby's portion? But the mother-love was too strong to disappoint her child.

"We'll see, Baby, we'll see when you are bigger."

They were too honest to promise even so vague a thing as this, merely to quiet the little one's whim.

It was still early for city folks to retire when Joe Perine opened the Bible and read a Psalm. Baby was nodding before the reading was finished. He stumbled through his "Now I lay me," and cuddled down in his poor little crib by his mother's bed. Opening his sleepy eyes a moment, he smiled up at her and put up his rosy lips for her good night kiss.

"Wot Chot, Jay Haut, Ta O-o," he murmured sleepily.

A little later the light went out in the Perine home, but somehow the mother could not sleep. Tired as she was with her long ride in the autumn air, and the excitement a trip to town brings to the humble country folk, her mind would not lose its grip on consciousness. The game, with its strange new appointments to her, kept picturing itself out again and again, and mingled with it was the thought of Baby. She reached out to his crib and felt his warm cheek and moist curls. He was so dear to her.

At length she fell asleep, and dreamed and dreamed. And always it was the same thing — the game, the hoarse college yell resounding in her ears, the struggle across the field, and mingled with it all was her own intense desire for her baby to go to school. And always the word came back: she must climb a high hill before her, first. That done, he could go to college. She tried to climb. She fell, but rose again, and stumbled on. Then she was at the game

Cuddy's Baby 15

again, and again she wished that her boy might go to college, and again the hill must be climbed.

In the pink light of dawn she awoke. Baby Harold had crept into bed beside her, and was softly kissing her cheek.

"Let me cuddle in wiz you. You is my own Cuddy. I'm doin' to have a vus'ty some day, ain't I, Mamma?" he said cooingly, and nestling in her arms he fell asleep.

II
The Cloud-Burst

II

THE CLOUD-BURST

Nobody knew how the fisherman brown,
With a look of despair that was half a frown,
Faced his fate on that fearful night,
Faced the mad billows with hunger white,
Just within hail of a beacon-light
That shone on a woman fair and trim,
Waiting for him.
—LUCY LARCOM.

THE May landscape was one deluge of green. For two weeks it had rained every day. Now and then a few hours of sunshine with a heavy steamy air had made life a burden to everything except the growing crops and faster growing weeds. Now and then the "clearing-up shower" of the rainy spell seemed to have fallen, and a red sunset gleamed feverishly in the west, only to be followed by an all-night rain. But for three days there had been no sunset. The sodden earth was chill; the creeks were running bank-full, and many a Kansas draw almost perennially dry was now a flooded stream, swift and fatally deceptive.

Joe Perine looked anxiously out from the doorway of the farm-house. Above the steady beat of the downpour he could hear a hoarse roar, the voice of the storm which no human voice may defy.

"It must be an awful rain to the west. Sounds like a cyclone or cloud-burst. They're gittin' it over in Grover township. An' what they git there they'll be sendin' here in a few hours. All the water off them little hills fills these draws in no time. Just listen, Mother!"

Mrs. Perine shook the flour from her hands, and, pushing aside her dough-pan, came and stood by her husband. A vague sense of insecurity possessed her, a dread of impending calamity hung over her. She was not a coward. The hard life of the home-builder in the West had given her a courage and a fearlessness in meeting danger. But this evening she looked imploringly at her husband as she caught the growl of that dreadful storm beating upon the helpless earth.

Joe smiled down at her and put one arm around her. All the love of a manly heart, all the hope and fearlessness of a courageous soul shone in his face, and drove her own fear away. She never forgot that moment. Long afterward it came to her in memory like a very benediction. Through lonely years, in days of deepest trials, it gave her, as at this moment, a new strength to meet whatever might come.

On the step at their feet sat Baby, staring out at the mad swirl of water where there never before had been anything but the draw between the pasture and the barnyard.

Baby was now nearly five, and while he was beginning to be a sturdy little boy, he was not quick to drop his baby speech, and he clung to his mother with an effusive love even for a child. "My Cuddy-Mamma," he had come to call her altogether now, keeping the pet name he had created, as little children will. And often it was just "Cuddy" alone that stood for all that "mother" can mean.

Since the day when he had seen with wondering eyes the student contest on the field by the roadside, he had many times come back to it in his childish prattle. Over and over in his mind he had turned this strange thing, so unlike any other impression there. Finally it became settled that the "vus'ty" was the best thing anybody could have. He had his own child-notion of what it meant, but there was the element of power in it. With it he could do anything, and its watchword was the college yell that in later years was to be heard all around the world.

For days together he would forget it, then suddenly he would break out with the jubilant cry. Especially had he come to answer his mother's call by it. So he had made known to her his hiding-places in the hay, and his little play-nooks about the rose-bushes. And when he was lost or afraid, his clear cry, half a defiance of fear and half a pleading for help, had come to be this University call. All children have such leadings along strange and unusual lines. Every mother knows how near the world of imagination and of quaint self-shaped ideas lies to the real world of the child. Every household has its set of phrases that the baby has created in some odd manner, phrases that need an interpreter to the stranger's ear.

And thus, far away from the great school, the noisy students' rallying, ringing slogan had become the watchword for protection, and power and loving assurance, for a tiny child in the poor little home of an ignorant farmer.

The rain that had poured in a torrent now ceased. The roar in the west had died down, but the sky was still one black shadow and there was a feeling in the air that the worst was yet to come.

"I must git the fences down and let the cattle into the upland before the creek gits any higher. The draw's risin' every minute," said Joe.

"Oh, Joe, I'm afraid for you to go." Mrs. Perine's face was white.

"Will you tum back, Papa?" asked Baby gravely.

"Well, I reckon I will," replied Joe gaily. "You take care of Cuddy-Mamma till I come. Deer Creek will reach clear over to the draw before mornin', an' if the cattle ain't let out there won't be no interest-money paid this year. We must save 'em."

They watched him go down the sodden way bordered with wet rosebushes and overhung with the rain-burdened branches of trees, his rubber boots splashing up drops at every step. Across the lot and into the draw he went, thinking, as they did, that the water would hardly cover his boot-tops. It reached nearly to his shoulders. They saw him tearing down the strong wire fence that separated the creek pasture from the upland. It was hard work, for the fence had been built to stay. The gates on the lower side of the field had been under water for two days.

Meanwhile there came a dull growl out of the west, an increasing, deepening roar — the sound of many waters. A darkness was dropping down on the land. Baby had slipped unnoticed into the house. The minutes seemed hours to the little woman by the kitchen door. A sense of utter loneliness seized her. She ran to the edge of the draw, straining her eyes to watch the moving figure across the meadow. The roar increased. A great surging stream came rushing from the west. It caught the cattle and their driver just as they tried to enter the draw, and swept them under in its wrath. A merciful darkness shut it all from the watcher on the hither side as the Death Angel passed down the way of the waters.

"Here, Mis' Perine, we'll take care of everything. You go back to the house to your baby. Little feller needs you now."

It was the kindly voice of Jake Basher, a big good-hearted neighbor, who spoke. Two or three other men were with him, rough Western farmers. but tender as ministering angels toward the dazed little woman suddenly stricken with a world-old grief.

"We'll be back pretty soon. You've got to be brave now, Lord help you. You've got your baby to think of. He'll be your blessin', too."

They hurried away, leaving behind them some sense of human aid.

It is a precious thing for us that underneath are always the Everlasting Arms, that when the earth goes out from under our feet in its place God comes. Mrs. Perine knew what had happened, and she turned toward the house.

The rain was over, and the May moon was lighting up the flood-smitten land with its splendor. Up the sodden way to the kitchen door, the over-hanging branches silvery with raindrops, and the fragrant roses strewing the path with perfumed petals,

Cuddy's Baby 25

she walked through her Gethsemane with the moonbeams falling like an aureole of glory about her. The kitchen was very dark, save for the square of light on the floor that fell through the open window. Baby was nowhere in sight, and the mother's heart was smitten with a new chill. What if he had followed her to the edge of that mad water and had fallen in when the terror of it all had driven her senses from her. She called to him. No answer came. She hastily lighted a lamp, calling again and again. Presently from the dark bedroom came a muffled voice, "Wock Chalk! Cuddy, Wock Chalk!" It was the little one's accustomed answer to her call, and climbing out from the bedclothes he ran to her with outstretched arms.

"I was so 'fraid," he said, clinging to her, "but I ain't now. I'll take care of you till Papa comes back."

Poor Mrs. Perine held him close to her heart.

"You are all I have now, Baby," she said.

His arms tightened about her neck.

"Let me cuddle up to you wite close. You is my Cuddy, an' I'll always love you. I'll not call you Mamma no more. You is ist my Cuddy."

To the grief-oppressed there is no love like the love of a little child, and no blessing like the blessing of toil. In the farm-house under the cottonwoods a new order of things had arisen. The work of the season, belated by the May floods, must go on. The loss of the cattle must be met. The mortgage interest did not quit growing, no more did the weeds. Ready money was only a dream. Hired help was hard to secure for a poor widow who could only promise to pay. Everybody needed help, for the rain had fallen on all alike. So it was hard times for Cuddy Perine and her child. The isolated farm-houses put miles of prairie between families, and hard work was combined with loneliness. It is only the truly heroic who can go through such tests and come out refined gold.

There was one blessing in all these things, however. There was no time for sitting idle, wrapped in a consuming grief. The sunshine that might have seemed a mockery to the mourner in a life of ease, meant ripening grain to the poor widow. The late summer rains that would bring back the memory of that awful May storm promised late pasture and better forage. And on these things depended Mrs. Perine's own existence and that of her beloved boy.

"Of course the Widder Perine 'll lose that hundred an' sixty. It's too bad Joe couldn't 'a' lived. I b'lieve he'd 'a' pulled through eventual. But she'd

Cuddy's Baby 27

better let the First National foreclose. She ought to move to town. She could do washin' an' keep herself some way."

So the good-intentioned neighbors declared. They would have helped her if they could, but they also had troubles to be met. It was this very good-will that had led them to gather at Jake Basher's house one bright Sunday afternoon in October to talk over what was best for their brave little neighbor making her struggle alone and single-handed. The consensus of opinion was that just expressed.

"It's too bad," they affirmed. "She's a plucky one, and willin' to work, but everything's agin her. An' the kindest thing the Deer Creek neighborhood can do fer her is to send a committee with Jake Basher fer spokesman an' tell her so. She'll never git through the winter."

So it was agreed that Jake Basher and two of his neighbors should go at once on this kindly errand. They found Cuddy and Baby Harold sitting on the doorstep. Cuddy's eyes were not on the grass-carpeted draw, where the tragedy of her life had been written, but up on the west ridge, where a dip in the hill pasture was revealing the last grandeur of an autumn sunset, tint on tint, like unto the foundation-stones in the walls of the New Jerusalem.

Gently as he could, for he was no

happy after-dinner speaker, Basher delivered their message.

"They ain't no other way fur ye to do, Mis' Perine. The other two reinforced their spokesman.

Cuddy's heart was like lead. She knew more than any of them what lay before her.

"I can't do it," she said. "If I go to town an' wash for a livin', there'll be nothin' but livin' to show for it. If I stay here there's something maybe besides just life. There's the farm—"

"But you can't keep it. You'll lose it, an' then where are ye?" So said one of the committee. "In a few years your boy kin hire out or git a job shovelin' dirt on the street. But you'd better have him bound out to some farmer. Farmers is always needin' bound-boys."

Cuddy looked down at the curly head beside her. A bound-boy! And herself a washerwoman. An honest worker, but little separated from the class who court pauperism. The face of her husband when he had given her that last caress, the bright brave face of Joe Perine, came to her at that moment. She lifted her eyes to the west where the sun, now gone from sight, was sending great shafts of pink far across the sky, like the arms of God reaching above the shadows of earth to lift her up.

"I'm so much obliged to you, but I'm goin' to stay an' fight it out," she said.

Cuddy's Baby 29

So the three left her. At the gate Jake Basher paused.

"You go on, an' I'll overtake ye. I've got to git me a drink. I'm dry as August."

He came back to the two on the doorstep. Baby's arms were about his mother's neck. He could not understand it all, but he knew vaguely, with a child's infinite trust, that there must be a way out.

"You shall stay here, Cuddy. I'm goin' to have a vus'ty when I'm big. I ain't goin' to be a bound-boy. An' when I get it I can do *any* fing." His voice swelled with the last sentence.

"You jest bet you can, little boy." There was a huskiness in Basher's voice, although he had no notion of what the child had in mind. "Keep this to help you get it."

He handed the little one a bright new penny.

"Now, Mis' Perine, you jest hang on. You're a gritty woman. Keep your nerve, an' don't give up. And whenever you git discouraged as you're bound to do," he pointed toward the dim outline of the divide far to the north, "you remember they's one family jest over Basher's hill that 'll stan' by ye tel — tel the las' dog's hung."

Then Basher rejoined his companions, and Cuddy and Baby were left alone.

"See, Cuddy," said Baby, holding up

Cuddy opened the old-fashioned clock and dropped the penny inside the case.

the bright penny. "It's to help get my vus'ty. Put it tight away."

Cuddy opened the old-fashioned clock and dropped the penny inside the case.

"It's the beginnin' for you, Baby," she said bravely. "It's small as could be, but it ain't no smaller than the little springs that begins the big rivers. 'An' the Lord, He it is that doth go before thee. He will not fail thee, nor forsake thee'," she added gently, and her voice sounded like a prayer.

Baby looked up with a childish reverence in his face.

III
Baby's Christmas

III

BABY'S CHRISTMAS

> You know
> How blessed 'tis to give.
> And they who think of others most
> Are the happiest folks that live.
> —PHŒBE CARY.

THAT was a bitter winter following the year of the heavy May rains in Kansas. The snows began early. Stock suffered greatly, even before Thanksgiving, while the December weather was more suggestive of a Michigan winter than the mild open Kansas month. The promise for a white Yuletide was sure.

Christmas is ever the same. There is no other good cheer in all the twelve months like the holiday gladness. There is no other giving such a joy as when the closing year brings again the Holy Night with its childish traditions of Santa Claus and its sacred, centuries-old benediction, "On earth peace; good-will toward men."

To the Kansas children Christmas was never more welcome, for to many it was their first snowy holidays, and they rejoiced in it with the mad joy of childhood.

Harold Perine's few toys had been Santa Claus gifts. No lavish array, to be sure. But with a little candy, a few nuts and an orange and some precious plaything, five times had his tiny stocking been filled. This year there must be a change. It was no use to deceive him with anticipations that could not be realized, his mother thought. It is brutal to rudely destroy this happy story of childhood, and yet she knew no Santa Claus would cross the snow to the home by the cottonwoods this year. With all his jolly love for children, the dear old saint has always most favored the little ones of the rich.

It was no small cross for Cuddy to find an excuse for this failure on his part. But she took it up as she was learning to lift all her crosses, one by one, bravely, even cheerfully. So one evening by the same old kitchen stove (they had only one fire, and fuel for that was growing scarce), she talked with her darling gravely about the case.

"He can't come every year, you know, and this may be his off year," she said.

"Why not? 'Cause we got no Papa?" queried Baby. "Will he be away in Papa's land?"

"No, dearie; there's better things than even Santa Claus where Papa is."

She had kept from him all the horror and grief of her tragedy. It had made her own sorrow lessen as she made beautiful to him the story of the Life Eternal into which his father had entered.

"What shall we do, Cuddy, wiv no Santa, I wonder?" he said thoughtfully. "Oh, I know, Cuddy, I know, I know." He danced about in his joy.

"Let's have ist one stockin', not yours nor mine, but Papa's for bof of us. Papa would ist love that, I know. An' I'll be your Santa, an' you be mine. It's ist all play until the year when he comes. Will that be the fat year like you read in the Bible 'bout Joseph and the 'Gyptians an bad old Pharaoh?"

"Yes, dearie, Santa will come again in the fat years. This is one of our lean ones. Lord help us!" she added under her breath. "An' we'll just play Santa Claus to each other. An' Papa will be glad we took his stockin', an' although we can't see him I am sure he will be near us on Christmas eve. But Baby, what shall I put in for you?"

"Oh, pwetty things."

"I haven't any. It's our lean year, you know. I wish I had." There were tears in her voice which Baby was quick to note.

"Never mind, 'Cuddy' " — and after a moment the cloud lifted for him. "Oh, Cuddy, you can't put a vus'ty in for me can you? Could you put a picture of a vus'ty, maybe? I'd ist like that so much."

"You must wait and see. What will you get for me?" she asked gaily.

"You must wait an' see," he replied quickly.

So they chatted of their Christmas, this lonely couple, building their holiday together. There was hardly a human need that was not theirs. Hunger, cold, toil, loneliness, and mourning — all were their daily portion; while there was no beauty in their home except the beauty of cleanliness, and pitifully few were the comforts of their household. But there was one thing plentiful there, and that was Love. Whatever else might fail, however sharp might be the pinch of poverty and the hard demands of labor, this best thing in the world stood firm. Cuddy's life was centered in her child. His mother was his idol. She kept a cheery heart for his sake, while he was already learning to do without things and to be self-reliant in his childish way, that he might not grieve his beloved.

On the day before Christmas the widow was obliged to go to town. It was too cold to take Baby. The pneumonia of past winters was not forgotten. It was a long afternoon trip, and to leave him alone seemed impossible.

"What shall I do with you?" Cuddy asked.

"I'll be good. I'll play an' keep close to the fire."

Cuddy's Baby

"But I'm afraid the fire will go out."

"Then I'll go to bed an' cuddle down to sleep."

"No, no; keep awake, whatever you do, so you can say 'Rock Chalk' when I come home and call you."

Visions of fire and of cold came to her, but she trusted as she must do most of the days now.

Early in the afternoon she started away on her long nine-miles drive to town. The north-wind swept drearily down the dull sky as she passed up the long way to the top of the divide. When she reached the grade by the field where the game had been played, the recollection of it filled her mind.

"My Baby's got to have learnin'," she said, closing her lips determinedly. "I can't give him nothin' else that will mean so much. The 'vus'ty' *is* power. It's better than money an' land, 'cause it puts the force *inside* and under his own control. These other things are *outside,* and maybe they'd control him. He can't never have a father nor brother nor sister. But he's got a mother's love an' he's goin' to get an eddication. An' they're blessin's that 'll shape his life. The Lord is good to let him have 'em."

Her heart thrilled with humble gratitude, and, as if to reassure herself, and drive away the cold as well, she clapped her mittened hands together and cried out cheerily:

"Rock Chalk! Jay Hawk! K. U.!"

Down on the main avenue the stores were gay with Christmas trappings, and tempting with toys and other delights. The show windows are always prettiest at the holiday season, but Cuddy could not stop to look at them, for time was precious, and the few pieces of silver in her purse must be used for debts that dogged her steps, or to fight back the wolf from her door.

"I can't even give him homemade candy," she said sorrowfully. Sugar and molasses were in her list of luxuries. "I wish I could find him a picture somewhere. His heart is so set on it."

The big bookstore of Basel & Company had never been more artistic in its holiday appointments. Crowded as it was, it had the atmosphere of a handsome library.

At a low counter young Basel, son of the proprietor, was attending a richly dressed woman who was buying lavishly for a little girl beside her.

"That will be all, will it, Mrs. Ancel?" he asked, turning to the next customer, against whom Mrs. Ancel stumbled as she started out.

It was only a shabby countrywoman, who stared about her, and Mrs. Ancel, sweeping past, gave her a look of infinite scorn.

"These country lubbers never look

Cuddy's Baby 41

where they are going when they get to town, Muriel," speaking to her little daughter. "They fill up a store so one can't shop. I wish they could be kept out of the city during the holidays."

Cuddy Perine shrank as from a blow. This place was too pretty for her, who so loved pretty things. Not three times in twice as many years had she been inside of a bookstore. Her meager reading had come from other sources. She turned to go now as one who had no right there.

"Can't I show you something?" It was young Basel's voice, courteously kind as it had been to the fine lady who had just passed out.

"I don't know," said Cuddy hesitatingly.

The young man understood at a glance. He was the spirit of this well-appointed bookshop that made it the pride of the town.

"Would you like to look about first?" She might have been the wife of a millionaire from his tone. It put a sense of self-respect into the widow's soul. How she would love to spend an hour there! But the little boy alone in the cold house — she must hurry.

"Have you any little cheap picture of the Kansas University?" she asked, fingering a precious silver dime in her coarse mitten.

Basel wondered afterward what kept him from fainting. She might as well have asked for an illuminated version of Herodotus, and not have surprised him more.

"My little boy wants one so bad," she said, seeing him hesitate as he put his hand on a pile of Mother Goose books.

"Yes, I think we must have. Come in here."

He led the way into an alcove where there were many pictures and stacks of illustrated pamphlets. Cuddy's eyes glistened as she looked about her.

"Here's a little lithograph. It's an advertisement of the University, but it's all we have."

It was a small souvenir-card showing the best of the University buildings, with hardly a hint at the magnificent landscape that lies about them. The grass was very green and the sky was very blue, for advertisements were not then the works of art they have since become.

"How much is it?" asked Cuddy.

"Oh, take it along. They were sent here in some catalogs of the school. Here, let me fix it up for your little one." He slipped it deftly into a small cheap frame made for holding photographs.

"Oh, thank you; much obliged to you. My Baby will be so glad."

"I wanted to give her something else

for her child," said Basel, speaking of it afterward. "But I didn't dare, somehow. There was that about her, shabby as she was, that wouldn't let me."

Cuddy tucked the precious picture safely away in her basket and started on her long homeward drive. The wind had gone down and a crisp frost-rimed world tinged with the clear purple and scarlet of a December sunset lay in winter stillness about her.

"It's lots warmer when you're happy," she said to herself. "Maybe Kansas ain't been very kind to me. But they's troubles wherever they's geography, I guess, an' somehow they's healin' to the soul in such a place as this." She breathed deeply of the bracing air, and her cheeks grew pink with its frosty caress. "I'd never want to live nowhere else now It's consecrated ground where your struggles is. Mine's here, heaven knows, but they ain't makin' me bitter nor selfish. Maybe it's because I can see so far. Back East a man can't even see all his own ground, let alone his neighbor's, an' he's apt to get the notion everything he sees is his an' part of what he don't see. He forgets all about the earth bein' the Lord's an' the fulness thereof."

Meanwhile, Baby Harold, left alone for the long hours of the afternoon, had tried every means he knew to kill time.

prairies, making fuzzy little snow-flurries along its path. The moonlight fell in a shower of silvery splendor, on a diamond-decked landscape. No reindeers and sleigh cut the long white road to the far-away cottage that night, but the trees stretched their arms in loving protection above it, and their shadows fell caressingly on roof and wall.

Cuddy sat late by the fire, mapping out her future step by step.

"I wonder," she mused, "if that fine lady in the bookstore loves her little girl any more than I love my boy, even if she could spend dollars, and I was glad of the gift for nothin'. She was such a pretty child, too, an' her name is Muriel. It's a sweet name. Some day, when Baby is dressed like a gentleman, I'd like to see him along-side such a girl. I won't think about her mother. I believe when my boy's grown up he'd rather have me poor an' kind than rich an' rude."

Cuddy's prayer that night was sweet and trustful.

"Dear Father," she prayed, "there's only one way before me, but it's Thy way. I don't know much, an' I can't do much myself. If I bring up my blessed Baby to be a strong man, an' to have schoolin', so's he can have a place in the world, an' to do good with the power that's his'n, take it, dear Lord, for my

Cuddy's Baby

gift to Thee. I know even if it seems like we just can't get through, that my hands is goin' to be strengthened; an' if I come to my burdens brave, they'll be like wings; when I lift 'em, they'll lift me. Give me hope an' courage an' love, so's I won't have bitterness an' hate in my heart, an' I'll fight my battle the best I can, until, some day, I can 'enter into Thy gates with thanksgivin,' an' into Thy courts with praise,' an' be with Joe again in Thy kingdom forevermore. Amen."

The world was magnificent that Christmas morning, done in ermine and mother-of-pearl, with a sunburst of radiance in the sky, and never a jagged line in all the soft, graceful curves of the snow-draped earth. Kansas had hardly known such a Canadian winter day among the milder holidays of its history. Long before Harold was awake his mother had made the kitchen warm and cosy. It was always clean, and this morning she would not stint the fuel. And since she was not only maid-of-all-work, but man-of-all-work as well, she had planned to have their celebration before she went to her cold task of milking, feeding and cutting the ice in the creek where the cattle might drink. There were only a few head saved out of that May flood, and they were very valuable now.

"What's in our stockin'? I ist can't wait!" cried Harold, tumbling pink and happy out of his morning sleep.

"Why, here's a picture, sure enough, and it's the University, too," said Cuddy.

Harold's cup was full. Years afterward, Muriel Ancel, speaking of that day, said, "I had so many gifts heaped on me that year I had no joy in any of them."

"And I had so few," Harold had replied, "that I had nothing but joy."

"It's a real vus'ty. A great big house, an' oh, pwetty grass an' everything like I dreamed last night. Tell me all about it."

He turned the picture about as though all Mount Oread lay at the back of the frame.

"Were you ever there, Cuddy?"

But Cuddy had found a bunchy little bundle of paper.

"Why, what can this be?"

Baby's eyes danced.

"It's my vus'ty penny, an' it's for you, Cuddy. It was all I had, an' it's ist for you."

How less than little it was, but the love that went with it meant millions. Cuddy understood both, the love and the sacrifice.

"It's to be the beginnin' of a Christmas 'vus'ty' fund, an' every Christmas, fat an' lean years, I'll add to it a little. An' when you grow up it will help to

Cuddy's Baby

pay your way to the 'vus'ty.' So there'll be something in Papa's stockin' for both of us."

"Will the vus'ty be yours, too, oh, Cuddy?"

"Yes, in a way, it will."

There was a jingling of sleighbells just outside the window, and Jake Basher's big kindly voice sang out, "Merry Christmas!" before Mrs. Perine could open the door.

"Ma sent me over to do your chores fur ye this mornin', and to bring some things ol' Santy lef' las' night by mistake," winking toward Harold. "Here's a pun'kin, an' some navy beans, an' some cookies, outlandishest things you ever seen — got baked into shapes like men an' horses an' things. An' some molasses candy, an' a few nuts. An' seein' it's so all-fired cold I jest hitched up to the bobsled. Ye see" — he hesitated — "a lot of drift-wood from the flood lodged down on the section below ye, an' as it wasn't rightly nobody's, the neighbors gethered it up an' cut it stove-lengths; an' as no one of 'em could take it they piled it on my bobsled yesterday fur me to bring in this mornin' to you. They's wood there they know is your'n, fur they ain't no other hick'ry trees on the creek except your farm here. They's four er five more loads, comin' in this week."

And there through the window Cuddy

caught sight of a wagon-bed on runners, piled high with seasoned wood, neatly corded.

"Why, when did you get it ready?" asked the surprised woman.

"The week after we was here in the fall an' you said you wasn't goin' to leave the farm, an' never put up no whine 'bout bein' a poor widder nuther," replied the farmer. "I'm lookin' fur an airly spring, an' they's wood to keep ye through."

Late that afternoon the mother and child sat together. In the latter's hand was his cherished picture.

"Tell me all 'bout it," he said.

"But I never was there."

"Well, tell me how you think it is," he persisted.

So Cuddy drew her own picture for him.

"I think it's up on a high hill like Basher's, because them that planned it first would know the value of not bein' crowded, and of havin' an outlook. A school's like a fort some ways — wants to overlook the country. An' I think there are lots more nice buildings there, all full of nice young folks, and they have good times and work hard. An' all around there's flowers and trees, where the scholars can sit an' study, or look off at the distance. It makes poets an' painters as well as scholars to go to the University, an' be where

Cuddy's Baby 51

they can learn an' where there's nothin' to shut off the skyline all around.

"I expect," she went on, "that they can see miles of farms an' orchards, and pastures, and maybe a river. The Kaw ain't very far from there. I 'most know they can see that; and then away off the soft purple where the earth and sky comes together. Think of watchin' a sunrise up there, an' of seein' all the pretty lights of evenin', an' in the fall after frost comes it must be glorious."

"Will I see it all some day?" asked Baby; "and what can I do wiv the vus'ty?"

"Baby, dear, you will see it. The University ain't easy to understand now. But you'll know when you get bigger. They's power in books, that can make you do good in the world. You can *be* good anyhow, but you can't *do* good, not much good, unless you have schoolin'. It begins over in the Deer Creek schoolhouse, but it don't never end, not even when you get a diplomy from the University."

Baby only half understood her words, but in the wisdom of his child-heart he caught the beginnings of what Life, real Life, means. Not always to those of mature years and wide opportunities alone is it vouchsafed to know the best things. In the mind of this little country boy the wisdom of the ages was finding lodgment. He never forgot that

Christmas day. Years afterward it seemed to him that he must have known intuitively then what he later went through many and various ways to justify.

When he said his "Now I lay me" that night, a sense of something hitherto unknown came upon him, and in the simplicity of his soul he added to his usual form: "Please make me a good boy, and — Dear Jesus, *I'm goin' to do it.*"

IV
Cuddy's Christmas

IV
CUDDY'S CHRISTMAS

Those who toil bravely and strongly,
  The humble and poor, become great,
And from these little brown-handed children
  Shall grow up mighty rulers of state.

THERE was a sameness about the years of the story that was writing itself out in the tree-sheltered home in the Deer Creek valley. Hard work, merciless economy, little leisure, many failures, many bitter discouragements marked the days. It was only a common-place life there, with no romance and no thrilling adventure; nothing to put into the poet's song, nor the fiction-writer's novel. Just a widow struggling to earn a livelihood, to keep down the gnawing debt that was eating at her land, to give her son what opportunities her meager resources afforded, and in her own patient, persistent way to grow into a larger mental life. And just a country boy to whom the commonest comforts were mostly luxuries — a boy — growing year by year toward a man's stature, with muscles like iron, a sound digestion, and, for anything he knew, no nervous system at all. His was an isolated life, and full of duties, but his buoyant good-nature and his innate eagerness for knowledge kept his spirit wholesome. Of necessity he learned how to sow and reap. He was wise in wood lore and prairie lore, and he gained skill in the use of such tools as he had. Of necessity he developed fearlessness and self-reliance. He fed horned cattle and handled vicious colts. He could swim like a fish, could climb to the highest places, and was surefooted in the narrow ways. He never lost his bearings. From the top of the west ridge Cuddy would catch his clear ringing "Rock Chalk! Jay Hawk!" which was always his signal to her, as down the dark lane he came singing home.

There were those who said Mrs. Perine had spoiled her boy, although they could excuse her on the ground of "havin' nothin' else to spoil." Yet they could but withdraw a little moral support from her when she stinted herself so one winter to pay for singing-lessons. Especially when Harry Perine went twice a week clear to town — nine miles — to take lessons of a city teacher, when Jennie Basher could play the organ and lead the choir and teach poor folks' children all the music they need to know. All Deer Creek neighborhood except Jake Basher declared "the Widder Perine was a fool, but a good-hearted one." Basher "didn't know but he'd 'a' done better to 'a' let Jennie had some more advantages." But the other neighbors set that down to Basher's modesty about his own girl.

But through all the shadow and shine of the seasons, the "vus'ty" notion of Baby Harold's childhood, growing slowly into the definite university idea, was never lost. Each Christmas eve the same old stocking hung by the kitchen chimney, and the penny fund grew slowly. The seasons fluctuated. Sometimes the "vus'ty" stock was at a premium, and sometimes it was desperately below par. But the fund was never used for any other purpose. It came to be the one feature of their holiday celebration, each trying to surprise the other by the size of the increase contributed. They might have grown miserly over it had its purpose been less generous. But always Cuddy kept before her boy the notion that education is a power for good or it is wasted energy.

Naturally they became students together, making use of every scrap of learning. It is wonderful how much the hungry mind can find to feed upon. One year an advertiser of liver pills issued a Shakespeare almanac with long quotations from Julius Caesar interspersed with glowing testimonials of restored liver-owners all the way from Molunkus, Maine, to Tarpon, Texas. It was in this almanac that Harold Perine and his mother found their Shakespeare. Something in Antony's eulogy of Brutus fastened itself in the boy's understanding.

> His life was gentle, and the elements
> So mix'd in him that Nature might stand up
> And say to all the world, "This was a man!"

The lines created an ideal for the boy that did not leave him.

And so they passed their days until the real University life began, and Harold Perine climbed the steep slope to the top of Mount Oread and saw the picture his mother had tried to paint in words on that Christmas afternoon so long ago.

The big, eager-hearted boy from the edge of the short-grass country brought to his new life a determined spirit, a sunny good-nature, and a manliness of character. But the order of the world seemed changed to him here. His first lesson was to discover that some students came with little intention of learning. It was a surprise to find how they squandered time and neglected opportunities. It was also a surprise to see how lavishly money could be spent by those who had never earned a dollar in their lives, and how much influence in University circles that money could bring. It was a revelation to discover how much of dissipation may creep into a college boy's life, unfitting him for the decent society in which he daily mingled. And the greatest surprise of all, the one he did not even mention in his letters to Cuddy, was that there could be such a beautiful girl outside of pictures as Muriel Ancel, whom he met on the day he entered school.

But he had grown up with one purpose, and he had lived too near to the heart of Nature, and the sweetness that comes up from the prairie sod of Kansas, and the inspiration that comes down from her splendid skies, were too much a part of his being, disciplined by years of endeavor, for him to lose his balance in the first bewildering whirl of his strange new life.

He knew at once that a battle was before him, the battle every poor boy must fight who attains to the mastery in the world of men. It was not a winning fight always, and only the remembrance of the patient mother at home, whose life, was his life, kept him sometimes from utter defeat. It is wonderful what Love can do. And how a plain little countrywoman, who had never been inside a college door, whose hands were unshapely from the tasks men perform, a woman of whom in the social sense one could not be proud — how this little mother, the Cuddy-Mamma of Harold Perine's babyhood — the companion of his childhood, was the inspiration of his manhood.

He filled his letters with all the University life he was living, until she came to know people and places and conditions almost as accurately as if she were a student herself. They had been happy companions at home. They were college chums now, and a new world opened for her — albeit it was only painted on note-paper with an indelible pencil.

"Oh, Cuddy," Harold wrote early in the first year, "it is tremendous just to be here, and to know the boys, and the girls. There's a girl here named Muriel, who is the prettiest girl in the world, I believe — except Cuddy, who is more than beautiful to me; and there are men whose very presence in the classroom puts self-respect inside a fellow, and make him take hold of things. You remember that poem we pasted on the clock-face, 'Each in His Own Tongue,' and how we loved the stanza:

> A haze on the far horizon,—
> The infinite, tender sky,—
> The ripe rich tint of the corn-fields,
> And the wild geese sailing high,—
> And all over upland and lowland
> The charm of the golden-rod —
> Some of us call it Autumn,
> And others call it God.

The man who wrote that is a professor here, and I know him personally. I never knew what hero-worship meant until I met him. Of course I know all

He filled his
letters with all
the University
life he was living.

about *saint-worship*. Learned that down on Deer Creek, where Saint Cuddy has a shrine."

So ran his letters in happy vein, carefully hiding the struggle-and-sacrifice side of things.

"She's had enough of that, heaven knows," he thought.

And his mother, with an unutterable loneliness added to her other cares, wrote only of the best things, hinting not at all of the conditions she had now to meet. His absence meant more than loneliness. His place must be filled, and Cuddy became her own hired help to save the money for his needs. One thing she had enforced upon him, and her letters repeated it: "You have only four years for the 'vus'ty' you have kept since childhood, Baby, and you must not put in all the time in study in school and hard work out of school. You may get through quicker, maybe, to crowd four years into three, but you are taking out of yourself what you put into your lessons. There's nothing, not even glory, in starving and slaving and studying. Get all you can out of books first, but don't forget to learn *how to fall in with folks* so you can take your place, not as a broken-down book-eater, but an all-round man. I'm too busy to nurse invalids, and you must keep strong, and if you graduate you don't want to be too awkward to know how to meet even the Governor of Kansas if you was introduced to him."

She added to this letter: "I never knew but one girl named Muriel, and that was when you was a baby. She was beautiful. It must be the name."

It is hard to tell which had the busier life, and it is useless to enter into the stress of it. Harold Perine came to his own at last, on the strength of intrinsic merit. There was no more popular fellow in the University than he. Even among the ultra-exclusive and the frivolous sets he was admired, while to every young student coming over the way he had come he was a tower of strength. He was the idol of the athletic field. The same spirit that years before had led him to cry out, "Wot Chot! Jay Haut! Ta O-o!" and so lead the University to conquest, had more than once brought victory to his comrades and honor to himself. His pride in the heavy course he was mastering, and his upright character, combined all with his own hopeful spirit, could but keep him in the very fore-front of the University life.

And naturally enough this was not Cuddy's life. It could not be, try as she would, for her own work must be done, and she knew she was filling her own place. So she did not grieve. She rejoiced, rather, sure of an unfailing love from her Baby. He never was anything else to her. Every vacation found him at home, falling easily into his place and lifting from his mother's shoulders all the burdens that he could. Every Thanksgiving and Christmas holiday his welcome call, "Rock Chalk! Jay Hawk!" would sound far down the valley from the top of the west ridge, to let his mother know that he was coming. They had no other signal that meant so much. Every Christmas-time the old stocking was hung in its place, and the big "Varsity athlete" put his best into it as years before he had concealed his blessed "vus'ty" penny.

One other thing had happened, the thing that has had a way of happening since the world was young. A new joy, that was unlike any other joy he had ever known; a happiness that made Mount Oread a delectable mountain glorified for him, had come to fill his days. Muriel Ancel, dark-eyed, pink-cheeked, sweet-voiced, with the gentleness of a child, and a spirit of exceeding kindness, had for three years been so much more than all else the spirit of the University for him. He had not told her so. He didn't know it himself for a long time, and when he did "find himself" the realization was more like pain than any sorrow he had ever known. There seemed to be a gulf ready to yawn between them as soon as Commencement should rob them

Cuddy's Baby 65

of more college days together, because their lives would be so widely divergent afterward.

When Harold met Mrs. Ancel he felt this more than ever, as he thought of Cuddy. "But I'd rather have my Cuddy poor and kind, than rich and rude," he had said to himself just as his mother had believed he would after the meeting in the bookstore in that earlier time. But Muriel was not like her mother, and Harold's heart was unchanged.

It came about that at the approach of the fourth Christmas of his school years a large house-party was planned in the Ancel home. A round of dinners and dances and rollicking good times was mapped out. Most of the guests were from Muriel's University set; and if anybody knows how to rig and launch a good time, a group of college boys and girls of many months' association together can do it. Music was to be a feature of every event. Muriel's touch on the piano was exquisite, and Harold's solos were to delight every company. His voice was now the fullness of that of which Joe Perine's voice was the promise. It had been his "open sesame" to the best musical circles. It took Harold a long time to write of all this to his mother, but when a man is in love there's only one face in the world for him.

His senior year was trebly expensive, of course, and the savings that would have almost sufficed for any other entire year were nearly exhausted by Christmas. Cuddy knew this, and she was planning how best to meet it. The mortgage was lifted now, and only half a year more of hard work and saving lay between her and her boy's Commencement, and then he would come home to her again, and take up the lines she might lay down.

The autumn had been full of discouragements when she most needed money, and her own strength was waning in a troublesome way. One dry fall day, just before Thanksgiving, a disastrous prairie-fire had swept over the west ridge and licked up every stack of her precious alfalfa; and a little later cholera broke out among the hogs. It seemed to Cuddy that money went to pieces before her eyes.

Added to this was an unusual loneliness and longing for her Baby's homecoming. She could hardly wait for the days to go by and Christmas eve to come.

Two days before Christmas, Jake Basher brought over the mail.

"Letter from your boy. Know'd ye'd want it. Reckon he'll be home tomorrow. It's turnin' cold. Looks like a blizzard getherin' up in the northwest, sweepin' in clear from Manitoby. Goodday, Mis' Perine, an' a Merry Christmas to ye." And he was off.

Cuddy's Baby

The letter was brief. It ran:

"DEAR CUDDY:—I've never been away from you at Christmas-time before, and I don't want to be now, but I'm invited to a house-party with a lot of our set, and I do want to go. You'll say 'yes,' Cuddy sweetheart, because you love your good-for-nothing Baby. I feel like Judas Iscariot to do it, but, Cuddy, I've got a girl who wants me to go—just like you must have asked my father years ago when you were pretty little Janet Meade, and Joe Perine was a young man like me. I've never been to her home yet, —just know her at school.

"You are the dearest Cuddy in the world, and I'll be home soon and tell you so.   Your loving
'BABY.'"

Cuddy sat long by the window with eyes that saw nothing. Her heart was sore. Her spirit bowed with the weight of disappointment. Never in all his twenty-two years had she risen on Christmas morning without her Baby to greet her. For seventeen years the same stocking hung on the chimney had served them both.

The day had been the one of the whole year when the peace of the angels' message to the shepherds out beyond Bethlehem had come into their hearts and made them rich in all good things.

"It's not because he's in love," Cuddy murmured half aloud. "I'd be a selfish mother to deny him the best thing in the world, though he don't even tell me her name nor where she lives; it's for him to be away at Christmas-time, when I'm so lonely, an' I need his advice about how to make up for the hogs and the alfalfa. But he don't know about that yet. I forgot that. Oh, dear, I just want him because I want him." She bowed her head on the kitchen table and the great hot tears fell upon it.

At last she stiffened bravely.

"You, poor, selfish old Cuddy, not to let your Baby, weighin' a hundred an' ninety pounds now, get away just one Christmas day. An' all them magazines he sent me to read, and so much to be done — I just can't get lonesome. An' I reckon if I do I can 'take it to the Lord in prayer' as I've done these many years, an' never been denied. *He* don't go 'way to spend Christmas. . . . . My! but it's gittin' cold. Basher's right about the blizzard."

The northwest was one gray-black frown, and a bitter air was penetrating every crevice with its sharp breath, although it was twenty-four hours before the blizzard in all its fury fell upon the Deer Creek valley.

Late in the next afternoon, Cuddy, who in spite of her efforts went perfunctorily about her tasks, had prepared her kitchen for the night. It was a foolish thing, she knew, but she could not resist the impulse to get out the old stocking and hang it as she had always done by the stove.

"He won't call 'Rock Chalk' to me this Christmas vacation, but I must do something for old times' sake," she said. "I've just had to imagine good things most of my life: I can do it a little more, I reckon."

The cold increased, and a blizzard from the northwest filled the air with its myriads of ice-needles. A whirl of blinding snow swept over the land so fiercely that all unprotected life in its pathway must perish before its wrath. It rattled at the widow's doors, and howled fiendishly about her roof.

And then she remembered what her disappointment and dulled senses had driven out of mind, namely, that the cattle must be gotten under shelter somehow. Without them the University year could not be completed. It was upon her to save them at any cost.

She hastily wrapped herself in cloak and hood, turning at the door to take one look at her warm, clean kitchen. It was such a cozy place at that moment! The stocking hung limp in its annual place of honor. Her chair by the window was inviting to a quiet rest. Harold's picture in football array leaned against the old clock on the shelf whence the "vus'ty penny" once came forth to fill a Santa Claus mission.

Should she let the cattle go and stay in this warm place? Then Joe Perine's face in its brave sweetness came back to her. So he had stood when the wrath of the Lord came down in the waters, and so he had gone out to do for her. She turned toward the cold outside.

"The draw's fillin' with snow now," she said, "an' it's gettin' dark; but I must save the cattle for my own that's left." And out into the storm's bewildering mazes she plunged, to do for one she loved.

No cold had ever chilled her so, as back and forth she struggled through the drifts. The stupid cattle were huddled in a sheltered corner in the far side of the pasture, and the snow was deepening about them. With frantic effort their rescuer tried to drive them toward the barn, wherein she meant to herd them until the storm was over. They broke away and ran back, they charged this way and that, wearing out the strength of their poor driver striving to save them.

At last they were safely gathered in and the door fastened, and Cuddy, numb with cold, started for the house. The snow blinded the way and all sense of direction was lost. Up the fatal draw she floundered, wondering why she could not find the gate. A drowsiness was creeping over her and she suddenly realized that she, too, was lost

Cuddy's Baby

in sight of her own home, just as her husband had been in the May flood eighteen years before. She roused herself for one more effort, but the snows of the draw only let her sink farther into their icy depths, and in that minute she lived again her whole life, moment by moment, up to this last supreme moment for which she waited.

The Ancel home was fairly aglow with Christmas wreaths, and beautiful in its luxurious furnishings, and gay with a host of jolly young folks just out of school, turned loose for a holiday vacation. It was high noon, and the train, a little behind-time, as trains will be at this season, had brought its last load of guests to this hospitable household.

At the doorway Muriel Ancel had just met the last comer, a handsome, tall young man, who did not enter.

"But, Harold, you promised me you'd stay with us," Muriel was saying, and there was no mistaking the disappointment in her tone. Nor was there any mistake about the expression in the dark blue eyes of the young man.

"Muriel," he said gently, "I was selfish when I promised. I wanted to come; so much I wanted to;" Muriel's eyes fell before his glance, "but I want more"—his hand closed gently over hers for a moment—"I want more to go home. There's a storm in the air; I can't tell you why, but I must go home."

The next moment he was gone. But the look as he turned away stayed with Muriel Ancel, just as his father's face had been a blesséd memory to the wife he loved.

Harold plunged off on his nine-miles walk as one whose feet had wings. He would not think of the beautiful home and the gay company of which he had had but a glimpse, a great impulse urged him on.

"I'm mighty glad," he said to himself, "that the wind is at my back. And I'm mighty glad I learned how to run on the football field, and how to walk mile after mile."

He beat his chest with his gloved hands and laughed aloud at the storm in the very vigor of youth and strength. But he had need for these. The storm increased and the cold grew with it.

"I never was lost in my life, just remember that, Old Mr. Blizzard," he cried gaily, trudging on his way.

But with all and all it was the longest nine miles he had ever tried to cover, and it was dark when he reached the west ridge — so dark he could have doubted had he not had the assurance of youth to carry him through. With every mile the Ancel home had faded from his desire, and the Perine home had grown until his very eagerness carried him on.

And then the
strong arms of her
blessed Baby
gathered her in ✦ ✦ ✦ ✦ ✦ ✦

Down in the snow-filled draw, Cuddy, fighting feebly against the blinding masses, was just at the moment of yielding to the drowsiness that makes that way out of life easy at last. A moment, when sweet and clear like an angel's silvery tone it seemed to her, came the ringing, cheery cry — the call that has been heard all round the world, from the rice-fields of the Philippines to the Arctic Circle off Greenland's coast:

"Rock Chalk! Jay Hawk! K. U.!"

Again and again it sounded. And Cuddy, with life once more in her grasp, fought fiercely at the drifts that clutched her feet. And then the strong arms of her blessèd Baby gathered her in, carried her through the draw, and up the white way to the kitchen door.

The cold was shut out, and in that little kitchen there was enough of "peace on earth and good-will to men" to have warmed the heart of the whole big world.

V
Christmas Bells

V

CHRISTMAS BELLS

IT WAS on a clear sweet Christmas afternoon that Harold Perine and Muriel Ancel were married in the quiet city church through whose stained windows a softened radiance of sunlight fell. The invited guests were all close personal friends, and every appointment of that wedding service was ideal. As the bride and groom entered the carriage to start on their nine-miles ride to the country home, the stone steps of the church suddenly filled with a crowd of old schoolmates from the University.

"Rock Chalk! Jay Hawk! K. U.!" they shouted in chorus again and again, until far down the street their voices died away and the two happy ones could hear them no more.

In the handsome new house on the west ridge Cuddy Perine waited once more her Baby's home-coming. It was the happiest hour of her life.

"My boy has come into his own kingdom at last," she said. "The 'vus'ty' he couldn't understand at first has brought him to be a man among men, and the whole State is proud of him.

He'll do better by his own children than I could do for him, but he couldn't have done it without me to help him to it. And the school did all the rest. It's more than money and land. Knowledge and judgment and a right conscience — that makes up real education. And now he's comin' home with the girl he's loved all these years. Seems like them that trusts in the Lord ain't goin' to want any good thing that He knows is good for 'em to have."

The carriage halted at the end of the long avenue leading up to the house, and once again the old college yell, first heard at the game so long ago, sounded across the prairie, a signal from Cuddy's Baby:

"Rock Chalk! Jay Hawk! K. U.!"